Faber
Stories

Edna O'Brien

Paradise

**Faber
Stories**

ff

First published in this single edition in 2019
by Faber & Faber Limited
Bloomsbury House
74–77 Great Russell Street
London WC1B 3DA
First published in *The Love Object* in 2013

Typeset by Faber & Faber Limited
Printed and bound by CPI Group (UK) Ltd, Croydon, CR0 4YY

A CIP record for this book
is available from the British Library

ISBN 978–0–571–35176–3

MIX
Paper from
responsible sources
FSC® C020471
www.fsc.org

10 9 8 7 6 5 4 3 2 1

In the harbor were the four boats. Boats named after a country, a railroad, an emotion, and a girl. She first saw them at sundown. Very beautiful they were, and tranquil, white boats at a distance from each other, cosseting the harbor. On the far side a mountain. Lilac at that moment. It seemed to be made of collapsible substance so insubstantial was it. Between the boats and the mountain a lighthouse, on an island.

Somebody said the light was not nearly so pretty as in the old days when the coast guard lived there and worked it by gas. It was automatic now and much brighter. Between them and the sea were four fields cultivated with fig trees. Dry yellow fields that seemed to be exhaling dust. No grass. She looked again at the four boats, the fields, the fig trees, the suave ocean; she looked at the house behind her and she thought, It can be mine, mine, and her heart gave a little somersault. He recognized her agitation and smiled. The house acted like a spell on all who came. He took her by the hand and led her up the main stairs. Stone stairs with a wobbly banister. The undersides of each step bright blue. 'Stop,' he said, where it got dark near the top, and before he switched on the light.

A servant had unpacked for her. There were flowers in the room. They smelled of confectionery. In the bathroom a great glass urn filled with talcum powder. She leaned over the rim and inhaled. It caused her to sneeze three times. Ovaries of dark-purple soap had been taken out of their wrapping paper, and for several minutes she held one in either hand. Yes. She had done the right thing in coming. She need not have feared; he needed her, his expression and their clasped hands already confirmed that.

They sat on the terrace drinking a cocktail he had made. It was of rum and lemon and proved to be extremely potent. One of the guests said the angle of light on the mountain was at its most magnificent. He put his fingers to his lips and blew a kiss to the mountain. She counted the peaks, thirteen in all, with a plateau between the first four and the last nine.

The peaks were close to the sky. Farther down on the face of the mountain various juts stuck out, and these made shadows on their neighboring juts. She was told its name. At the same moment she overheard a question being put to a young woman, 'Are you interested in Mary Queen of Scots?' The woman, whose skin had a beguiling radiance, answered yes overreadily. It was possible that such radiance was the result of constant supplies of male sperm. The man had a high pale forehead and a look of death.

They drank. They smoked. All twelve smokers tossing the butts onto the tiled roof that sloped toward the farm buildings. Summer lightning started up. It was random and quiet and faintly theatrical. It seemed to be something devised for their amusement. It lit one part of the sky, then another. There were bats flying about also, and their dark shapes and the random fugitive shots of summer lightning were a distraction and gave them something to point to. 'If I had a horse I'd

3

call it Summer Lightning,' one of the women said, and the man next to her said, How charming. She knew she ought to speak. She wanted to. Both for his sake and for her own. Her mind would give a little leap and be still and would leap again; words were struggling to be set free, to say something, a little amusing something to establish her among them. But her tongue was tied. They would know her predecessors. They would compare her minutely, her appearance, her accent, the way he behaved with her. They would know better than she how important she was to him, if it were serious or just a passing notion. They had all read in the gossip columns how she came to meet him; how he had gone to have an X-ray and met her there, the radiographer in white, committed to a dark room and films showing lungs and pulmonary tracts.

'Am I right in thinking you are to take swimming lessons?' a man asked, choosing the moment when she had leaned back and was staring up at a big pine tree.

'Yes,' she said, wishing that he had not been told.

'There's nothing to it, you just get in and swim,' he said.

How surprised they all were, surprised and amused. Asked where she had lived and if it was really true.

'Can't imagine anyone not swimming as a child.'

'Can't imagine anyone not swimming, period.'

'Nothing to it, you just fight, fight.'

The sun filtered by the green needles fell and made play on the dense clusters of brown nuts. They never ridicule nature, she thought, they never dare. He came and stood behind her, his hand patting her bare pale shoulder. A man who was not holding a camera pretended to take a photograph of them. How long would she last? It would be uppermost in all their minds.

'We'll take you on the boat tomorrow,' he said. They cooed. They all went to such pains, such excesses, to describe the cruiser. They competed with each other to tell her. They were really telling him. She thought, I should be honest, say I do not like the sea, say I am an inland person, that I like rain

5

and roses in a field, thin rain, and through it the roses and the vegetation, and that for me the sea is dark as the shells of mussels, and signifies catastrophe. But she couldn't.

'It must be wonderful' was what she said.

'It's quite, quite something,' he said shyly.

At dinner she sat at one end of the egg-shaped table and he at the other. Six white candles in glass sconces separated them. The secretary had arranged the places. A fat woman on his right wore a lot of silver bracelets and was veiled in crepe. They had cold soup to start with. The garnishings were so finely chopped that it was impossible to identify each one except by its flavor. She slipped out of her shoes. A man describing his trip to India dwelt for an unnaturally long time on the disgustingness of the food. He had gone to see the temples. Another man, who was repeatedly trying to buoy them up, threw the question to the table at large: 'Which of the Mediterranean ports is best to dock at?' Everyone had a favorite. Some picked ports where exciting things had happened, some chose ports where the approach was most beguiling, harbor fees were compared as a matter of interest; the man who had asked the question amused them all with an account of a cruise he had made once with his young daughter and of how he was unable to land when they got to Venice because of inebriation. She had to admit that she did not know any ports. They were touched by that confession.

'We're going to try them all,' he said from the opposite end of the table, 'and keep a logbook.' People looked from him to her and smiled knowingly.

That night behind closed shutters they enacted their rite. They were both impatient to get there. Long before the coffee had been brought they had moved away from the table and contrived to be alone, choosing the stone seat that girdled the big pine tree. The seat was smeared all over with the tree's transparent gum. The nuts bobbing together made a dull clatter like castanets. They sat for as long as courtesy required, then they retired. In bed she felt safe again, united to him not only by passion and by pleasure but by some more radical entanglement. She had no name for it, that puzzling emotion that was more than love, or perhaps less, that was not simply sexual, although sex was vital to it and held it together like wires supporting a broken bowl. They both had had many breakages and therefore loved with a wary superstition.

'What you do to me,' he said. 'How you know me, all my vibrations.'

'I think we are connected underneath,' she said quietly. She often thought he hated her for implicating him in something too tender. But he was not hating her then.

At length it was necessary to go back to her bedroom, because he had promised to get up early to go spearfishing with the men.

As she kissed him goodbye she caught sight of herself in the chrome surface of the coffee flask which was on his bedside table – eyes emitting satisfaction and chagrin and panic were what stared back at her. Each time as she left him she expected not to see him again; each parting promised to be final.

The men left soon after six; she heard car doors because she had been unable to sleep.

In the morning she had her first swimming lesson. It was arranged that she would take it when the others sat down to breakfast. Her instructor had been brought from England. She asked if he'd slept well. She did not ask where. The servants disappeared from the house late at night and departed toward the settlement of low-roofed buildings. The dog went with them. The instructor told her to go backward down the metal stepladder. There were wasps hovering about and she thought that if she were to get stung she could bypass the lesson. No wasp obliged.

Some children, who had been swimming earlier, had left their plastic toys – a yellow ring that craned into the neck and head of a duck. It was a duck with a thoroughly disgusted expression. There was as well a blue dolphin with a name painted on it, and all kinds of battleships. They were the children of guests. The older ones, who were boys, took no notice of any of the adults and moved about, raucous and meddlesome, taking full advantage of every aspect of the place – at night they watched the lizards patiently and for hours, in the heat of the day they remained in the water, in the early morning they gathered almonds, for which they received from him a harvesting fee. One black flipper lurked on the bottom of the pool. She looked down at it and touched it with her toe. Those were her last unclaimed moments, those moments before the lesson began.

The instructor told her to sit, to sit in it, as if it were a bath. He crouched and slowly she crouched, too. 'Now hold your nose and put your head under water,' he said. She pulled the bathing cap well over her ears and forehead to protect her hairstyle, and with her nose gripped too tightly she went underneath. 'Feel it?' he said excitedly. 'Feel the water holding you up?' She felt no such thing. She felt the water engulfing her. He told her to press the water from her eyes. He was gentleness itself. Then he dived in, swam a few strokes, and stood up, shaking the water from his gray hair. He took her hands and walked backward until they were at arm's length. He asked her to lie on her stomach and give herself to it. He promised not to let go of her hands. Each time, on the verge of doing so, she stopped: first her body, then her mind refused. She felt that if she was to take her feet off the ground the unmentionable would happen. 'What do I fear?' she asked herself. 'Death,' she said, and yet, it was not that. It was as if some horrible experience would happen before her actual death. She thought perhaps it might be the fight she would put up.

When she succeeded in stretching out for one desperate minute, he proclaimed with joy. But that first lesson was a failure as far as she was concerned. Walking back to the house, she realized it was a mistake to have allowed an instructor to be brought. It put too much emphasis on it. It would be incumbent upon her to conquer it. They would concern themselves with her progress, not because they cared, but like the summer lightning or the yachts going by, it would be something to talk about. But she could not send the instructor home. He was an old man and he had never been abroad before. Already he was marveling at the scenery. She had to go on with it. Going back to the terrace, she was not sure of her feet on land, she was not sure of land itself; it seemed to sway, and her knees shook uncontrollably.

When she sat down to breakfast she found that a saucer of almonds had been peeled for her. They were sweet and fresh, reinvoking the sweetness and freshness of a country morning. They tasted like hazelnuts. She said so. Nobody agreed. Nobody disagreed. Some were reading papers. Now and then someone read a piece aloud, some amusing piece about some acquaintance of theirs who had done a dizzy, newsworthy thing. The children read the thermometer and argued about the penciled shadow on the sundial. The temperature was already in the eighties. The women were forming a plan to go on the speedboat to get their midriffs brown. She declined. He called her into the conservatory and said she might give some time to supervising the meals because the secretary had rather a lot to do.

Passion-flower leaves were stretched along the roof on lifelines of green cord. Each leaf like the five fingers of a hand. Green and yellow leaves on the same hand. No flowers. Flowers later. Flowers that would live a day. Or so the gardener had said. She said, 'I hope we will be here to see one.' 'If you want, we will,' he said, but of course he might take a notion and go. He never knew what he might do; no one knew.

When she entered the vast kitchen, the first thing the servants did was to smile. Women in black, with soft-soled shoes, all smiling, no complicity in any of those smiles. She had brought with her a phrase book, a notebook, and an English cookery book. The kitchen was like a laboratory – various white machines stationed against the walls, refrigerators churtling at different speeds, a fan over each of the electric cookers, the red and green lights on the dials faintly menacing, as if they were about to issue an alarm. There was a huge fish on the table.

It had been speared that morning by the men. Its mouth was open; its eyes so close together that they barely missed being one eye; its lower lip gaping pathetically. The fins were black and matted with oil. They all stood and looked at it, she and the seven or eight willing women to whom she must make herself understood. When she sat to copy the recipe from the English book and translate it into their language, they turned on another fan. Already they were chopping for the evening meal. Three young girls chopped onions, tomatoes, and peppers. They seemed to take pleasure in their tasks; they seemed to smile into the mounds of vegetable that they so diligently chopped.

There were eight picnic baskets to be taken on the boat. And armfuls of towels. The children begged to be allowed to carry the towels. He had the zip bag with the wine bottles. He shook the bag so that the bottles rattled in their surrounds of ice. The guests smiled. He had a way of drawing people into his mood without having to say or do much. Conversely he had a way of locking people out. Both things were mesmerizing. They crossed the four fields that led to the sea. The figs were hard and green. The sun played like a blow lamp upon her back and neck. He said that she would have to lather herself in suntan oil. It seemed oddly hostile, his saying it out loud like that, in front of the others. As they got nearer the water she felt her heart race. The water was all shimmer. Some swam out, some got in the rowboat. Trailing her hand in the crinkled surface of the water she thought, It is not cramp, jellyfish, or broken glass that I fear, it is something else. A ladder was dropped down at the side of the boat for the swimmers to climb in from the sea. Sandals had to be kicked off as they stepped inside. The floor was of blond wood and burning hot. Swimmers had to have their feet inspected for tar marks. The boat-man stood with a pad of cotton soaked in turpentine ready to rub the marks. The men busied themselves – one helped to get the engine going, a couple put awnings up, others carried out large striped cushions and scattered them under the awnings. Two boys refused to come on board.

'It is pleasant to bash my little brother up under water,' a young boy said, his voice at once menacing and melodious.

She smiled and went down steps to where there was a kitchen and sleeping quarters with beds for four. He followed her. He looked, inhaled deeply, and murmured.

'Take it out,' she said, 'I want it now, now.' Timorous and whim mad. How he loved it. How he loved that imperative. He pushed the door and she watched as he struggled to take down his shorts but could not get the cord undone. He was the awkward one now. How he stumbled. She waited for one excruciating moment and made him wait. Then she knelt, and as she began he muttered between clenched teeth. He who could tame animals was defenseless in this. She applied herself to it, sucking, sucking, sucking, with all the hunger that she felt and all the simulated hunger that she liked him to think she felt. Threatening to maim him, she always just grazed with the edges of her fine square teeth. Nobody intruded. It took no more than minutes. She stayed behind for a decent interval. She felt thirsty. On the window ledge there were paperback books and bottles of sun oil. Also a spare pair of shorts that had names of all the likely things in the world printed on them – names of drinks and capital cities and the flags of each nation. The sea through the porthole was a small, harmless globule of blue.

They passed out of the harbor, away from the three other boats and the settlement of pines. Soon there was only sea and rock, no reedy inlets, no towns. Mile after mile of hallucinating sea. The madness of mariners conveyed itself to her, the illusion that it was land and that she could traverse it. A land that led to nowhere. The rocks had been reduced to every shape the eye and the mind could comprehend. Near the water there were openings that had been forced through by the sea – some rapacious, some large enough for a small boat to slink in under, some as small and unsettling as the sockets of eyes. The trees on the sheer faces of these rocks were no more than the struggle to be trees. Birds could not perch there, let alone nest. She tried not to remember the swimming lesson, to postpone remembering until the afternoon, until the next lesson.

She came out and joined them. A young girl sat at the stern, among the cushions, playing a guitar. She wore long silver spatula-shaped earrings. A self-appointed gypsy. The children were playing I Spy but finding it hard to locate new objects. They were confined to the things they could see around them. By standing she found that the wind and the spray from the water kept her cool. The mountains that were far away appeared insubstantial, but those that were near glinted when the sharp stones were pierced by the sun.

'I find it a little unreal,' she said to one of the men. 'Beautiful but unreal.' She had to shout because of the noise of the engine.

'I don't know what you mean by unreal,' he said.

Their repertoire was small but effective. In the intonation the sting lay. Dreadfully subtle. Impossible to bridle over. In fact, the unnerving thing about it was the terrible bewilderment it induced. Was it intended or not? She distinctly remembered a sensation of once thinking that her face was laced by a cobweb, but being unable to feel it with the hand and being unable to put a finger on their purulence felt exactly the same. To each other, too, they transmitted small malices and then moved on to the next topic. They mostly talked of places they had been to and the people who were there, and though they talked endlessly, they told nothing about themselves.

They picnicked on a small pink strand. He ate very little, and afterward he walked off. She thought to follow him, then didn't. The children waded out to sea on a long whitened log, and one of the women read everybody's hand. She was promised an illness. When he returned he gave his large yellowish hand reluctantly. He was promised a son. She looked at him for a gratifying sign but got none. At that moment he was telling one of the men about a black sloop that he had loved as a child. She thought, What is it that he sees in me, he who loves sea, sloops, jokes, masquerades, and deferment?

What is it that he sees in me who loves none of those things?

Her instructor brought flat white boards. He held one end, she the other. She watched his hands carefully. They were very white from being in water. She lay on her stomach and held the boards and watched his hands in case they should let go of the board. The boards kept bobbing about and adding to her uncertainty. He said a rope would be better.

The big fish had had its bones removed and was then pieced together. A perfect decoy. Its head and its too near eyes were gone. On her advice the housekeeper had taken the lemons out of the refrigerator, so that they were like lemons now rather than bits of frozen sponge. Someone remarked on this and she felt childishly pleased. Because of a south wind a strange night exhilaration arose. They drank a lot. They discussed beautiful evenings. Evenings resurrected in them by the wine and the wind and a transient goodwill. One talked of watching golden cock pheasants strutting in a back yard; one talked of bantams perched on a gate at dusk, their forms like notes of music on a blank bar; no one mentioned love or family, it was scenery or nature or a whippet that left them with the best and most serene memories. She relived a stormy night with an ass braying in a field and a blown bough fallen across a road. After dinner various couples went for walks, or swims, or to listen for children. The three men who were single went to the village to reconnoiter. Women confided the diets they were on, or the face creams that they found most beneficial. A divorcée said to her host, 'You've *got* to come to bed with me, you've simply *got* to,' and he smiled. It was no more than a pleasantry, another remark in a strange night's proceedings where there were also crickets, tree frogs, and the sounds of clandestine kissing. The single men came back presently and reported that the only bar was full of Germans and that the whiskey was inferior. The one who had been most scornful about her swimming sat at her feet and said how awfully pretty she was. Asked her details about

21

her life, her work, her schooling. Yet this friendliness only reinforced her view of her own solitude, her apartness. She answered each question carefully and seriously. By answering she was subscribing to her longing to fit in. He seemed a little jealous, so she got up and went to him. He was not really one of them, either. He simply stage-managed them for his own amusement. Away from them she almost reached him. It was as if he were bound by a knot that maybe, maybe, she could unravel, for a long stretch, living their own life, cultivating a true emotion, independent of other people. But would they ever be away? She dared not ask. For that kind of discussion she had to substitute with a silence.

She stole into their rooms to find clues to their private selves – to see if they had brought sticking plaster, indigestion pills, face flannels, the ordinary necessities. On a dressing table there was a wig block with blond hair very artfully curled. On the face of the block colored sequins were arranged to represent the features of an ancient Egyptian queen. The divorcée had a baby's pillow in a yellow muslin case. Some had carried up bottles of wine and these though not drunk were not removed. The servants only touched what was thrown on the floor or put in the waste-paper baskets. Clothes for washing were thrown on the floor. It was one of the house rules, like having cocktails on the terrace at evening time. Some had written cards which she read eagerly. These cards told nothing except that it was all super.

His secretary, who was mousy, avoided her. Perhaps she knew too much. Plans he had made for the future.

She wrote to her doctor:

I am taking the tranquillizers but I don't feel any more relaxed. Could you send me some others?

She tore it up.

Her hair got tangled by the salt in the sea air. She bought some curling tongs.

One woman, who was pregnant, kept sprinkling baby powder and smoothing it over her stomach throughout the day. They always took tea together. They were friends. She thought, If this woman were not pregnant would she be so amiable? Their kind of thinking was beginning to take root in her.

The instructor put a rope over her head. She brought it down around her middle. They heard a quack-quack. She was certain that the plastic duck had intoned. She laughed as she adjusted the noose. The instructor laughed, too. He held a firm grip of the rope. She threshed through the water and tried not to think of where she was. Sometimes she did it well; sometimes she had to be brought in like an old piece of lumber. She could never tell the outcome of each plunge; she never knew how it was going to be or what thoughts would suddenly obstruct her. But each time he said, 'Lovely, lovely,' and in his exuberance she found consolation.

A woman called Iris swam out to their yacht. She dangled in the water and with one hand gripped the sides of the boat. Her nail varnish was exquisitely applied and the nails had the glow of a rich imbued pearl. By contrast with the pearl coating, the half-moons were chastely white. Her personality was like that, too – full of glow. For each separate face she had a smile, and a word or two for those she already knew. One of the men asked if she was in love. Love! she riled him. She said her good spirits were due to her breathing. She said life was a question of correct breathing. She had come to invite them for drinks but he declined because they were due back at the house. His lawyer had been invited to lunch. She chided him for being so busy, then swam off toward the shore, where her poodle was yapping and waiting for her. At lunch they all talked of her. There was mention of her past escapades, the rows with her husband, his death, which was thought to be a suicide, and the unpleasant business of his burial, which proved impossible on religious grounds. Finally, his body had to be laid in a small paddock adjoining the public cemetery. Altogether an unsavory story, yet preening in the water had been this radiant woman with no traces of past harm.

'Yes, Iris has incredible willpower, incredible,' he said.

'For what?' she asked, from the opposite end of the table.

'For living,' he said tartly.

It was not lost on the others. Her jaw muscle twitched.

Again she spoke to herself, remonstrated with her hurt: 'I try, I try, I want to fit, I want to join, be the someone who slips into a crowd of marchers when the march has already begun, but there is something in me that I call sense and it balks at your ways. It would seem as if I am here simply to smart under your strictures.' Retreating into dreams and monologue.

She posed for a picture. She posed beside the sculptured lady. She repeated the pose of the lady. Hands placed over each other and laid on the left shoulder, head inclining toward those hands. He took it. Click, click. The marble lady had been the sculptor's wife and had died tragically. The hands with their unnaturally long nails were the best feature of it. Click, click. When she was not looking he took another.

She found the account books in a desk drawer and was surprised at the entries. Things like milk and matches had to be accounted for. She thought, Is he generous at the roots? The housekeeper had left some needlework in the book. She had old-fashioned habits and resisted much of the modern kitchen equipment. She kept the milk in little pots, with muslin spread over the top. She skimmed the cream with her fat fingers, tipped the cream into small jugs for their morning coffee. What would they say to that! In the evenings, when every task was done, the housekeeper sat in the back veranda with her husband, doing the mending. They had laid pine branches on the roof, and these had withered and were tough as wire. Her husband made shapes from soft pieces of new white wood, and then in the dark put his penknife aside and caroused with his wife. She heard them when she stole in to get some figs from the refrigerator. It was both poignant and untoward.

The instructor let go of the rope. She panicked and stopped using her arms and legs. The water was rising up over her. The water engulfed her. She knew that she was screaming convulsively. He had to jump in, clothes and all. Afterward they sat in the linen room with a blanket each and drank brandy. They vouched to tell no one. The brandy went straight to his head. He said in England it would be raining and people would be queueing for buses, and his eyes twinkled because of his own good fortune at being abroad.

More than one guest was called Teddy. One of the Teddys told her that in the mornings before his wife wakened he read Proust in the dressing room. It enabled him to masturbate. It was no more than if he had told her he missed bacon for breakfast.

For breakfast there was fruit and scrambled egg. Bacon was a rarity on the island. She said to the older children that the plastic duck was psychic and had squeaked. They laughed. Their laughing was real, but they kept it up long after the joke had expired. A girl said, 'Shall I tell you a rude story?' The boys appeared to want to restrain her. The girl said, 'Once upon a time there was a lady, and a blind man came to her door every evening for sixpence, and one day she was in the bath and the doorbell rang and she put on a gown and came down and it was the milkman, and she got back in the bath and the doorbell rang and it was the bread man, and at six o'clock the doorbell rang and she thought, I don't have to put on my gown it is the blind man, and when she opened the door the blind man said, "Madam, I've come to tell you I got my sight back."' And the laughter that had never really died down started up again, and echoed. No insect, no singing bird was heard on that walk. She had to watch the time. The children's evening meal was earlier. They ate on the back veranda and she often went there and stole an anchovy or a piece of bread so as to avoid getting too drunk before dinner. There was no telling how late dinner would be. It depended on him, on whether he was bored or not. Extra guests from neighboring houses came each evening for drinks. They added variety. The talk was about sailing and speeding, or about gardens, or about pools. They all seemed to be intrigued by these topics, even the women. One man who followed the snow knew where the best snow surfaces were for every week of every year. That subject did not bore her as much. At least the snow was nice to think about, crisp and blue like he said, and rasping under the skis. The children could often be heard shrieking, but after cocktail hour they never appeared. She believed that it would be better once they were married and had children. She would be accepted by courtesy of them. It was a swindle really, the fact that small creatures, ridiculously easy to beget, should solidify a relationship, but they would. Everyone hinted how he wanted a son. He was nearing sixty. She had stopped using contraceptives and he had stopped asking. Perhaps that was his way of deciding, of finally accepting her.

Gulls' eggs, already shelled, were brought to table. The yolks a very delicate yellow. 'Where are the shells?' the fat lady, veiled in crepe, asked. The shells had to be brought. They were crumbled almost to a powder but were brought anyhow. 'Where are the nests?' she asked. It missed. It was something they might have laughed at, had they heard, but a wind had risen and they were all getting up and carrying things indoors. The wind was working up to something. It whipped the geranium flowers from their leaves and crazed the candle flames so that they blew this way and that in the glass sconces. That night their lovemaking had all the sweetness and all the release that earth must feel with the long-awaited rain. He was another man now, with another voice – loving and private and incantatory. His coldness, his dismissal of her hard to believe in. Perhaps if they quarreled, their quarrels, like their lovemaking, would bring them closer. But they never did. He said he'd never had a quarrel with any of his women. She gathered that he left his wives once it got to that point. He did not say so, but she felt that must have been so, because he had once said that all his marriages were happy. He said there had been fights with men but that these were decent. He had more rapport with men; with women he was charming but it was a charm devised to keep them at bay. He had no brothers, and no son. He had had a father who bullied him and held his inheritance back for longer than he should. This she got from one of the men who had known him for forty years. His father had caused him to suffer, badly. She did not know in what way and she was unable to ask him, because it was information she should never have been given a hint of.

After their trip to the Roman caves the children came home ravenous. One child objected because the meal was cold. The servant, sensing a certain levity, told her master, and the story sent shrieks of laughter around the lunch table. It was repeated many times. He called to ask if she had heard. He sometimes singled her out in that way. It was one of the few times the guests could glimpse the bond between them. Yes, she had heard. 'Sweet, sweet,' she said. The word occurred in her repertoire all the time now. She was learning their language. And fawning. Far from home, from where the cattle grazed. The cattle had fields to roam, and a water tank near the house. The earth around the water tank always churned up, always mucky from their trampling there. They were farming people, had their main meal in the middle of the day, had rows. Her father vanished one night after supper, said he was going to count the cattle, brought a flashlamp, never came back. Others sympathized, but she and her mother were secretly relieved. Maybe he drowned himself in one of the many bog lakes, or changed his name and went to a city. At any rate, he did not hang himself from a tree or do anything ridiculous like that.

She lay on her back as the instructor brought her across the pool, his hand under her spine. The sky above an innocent blightless blue, with streamers where the jets had passed over. She let her head go right back. She thought, If I were to give myself to it totally, it would be a pleasure and an achievement, but she couldn't.

Argoroba hung from the trees like blackened banana skins. The men picked them in the early morning and packed them in sacks for winter fodder. In the barn where these sacks were stored there was a smell of decay. And an old olive press. In the linen room next door a pleasant smell of linen. The servants used too much bleach. Clothes lost their sharpness of color after one wash. She used to sit in one or another of these rooms and read. She went to the library for a book. He was in one of the Regency chairs that was covered with ticking. As on a throne. One chair was real and one a copy, but she could never tell them apart. 'I saw you yesterday, and you nearly went under,' he said. 'I still have several lessons to go,' she said, and went as she intended, but without the book that she had come to fetch.

—

His daughter by his third marriage had an eighteen-inch waist. On her first evening she wore a white trouser suit. She held the legs out, and the small pleats when opened were like a concertina. At table she sat next to her father and gazed at him with appropriate awe. He told a story of a dangerous leopard hunt. They had lobster as a special treat. The lobster tails, curving from one place setting to the next, reached far more cordially than the conversation. She tried to remember something she had read that day. She found that by memorizing things she could amuse them at table.

'The gorilla resorts to eating, drinking, or scratching to bypass anxiety,' she said later. They all laughed.

'You don't say,' he said, with a sneer. It occurred to her that if she were to become too confident he would not want that, either. Or else he had said it to reassure his daughter.

There were moments when she felt confident. She knew in her mind the movements she was required to make in order to pass through the water. She could not do them, but she knew what she was supposed to do. She worked her hands under the table, trying to make deeper and deeper forays into the atmosphere. No one caught her at it. The word 'plankton' would not let go of her. She saw dense masses of it, green and serpentine, enfeebling her fingers. She could almost taste it.

His last wife had stitched a backgammon board in green and red. Very beautiful it was. The fat woman played with him after dinner. They carried on the game from one evening to the next. They played very contentedly. The woman wore a different arrangement of rings at each sitting and he never failed to admire and compliment her on them. To those not endowed with beauty he was particularly charming.

Her curling tongs fused the entire electricity system. People rushed out of their bedrooms to know what had happened. He did not show his anger, but she felt it. Next morning they had to send a telegram to summon an electrician. In the telegram office two men sat, one folding the blue pieces of paper, one applying gum with a narrow brush and laying thin borders of white over the blue and pressing down with his hands. On the white strips the name and address had already been printed. A motorcycle was indoors, to protect the tires from the sun, or in case it might be stolen. The men took turns when a telegram had to be delivered. She saved one or the other of them a journey because a telegram from a departed guest arrived while she was waiting. It simply said 'Adored it, Harry.' Guests invariably forgot something and in their thank-you letters mentioned what they had forgotten. She presumed that some of the hats stacked into one another and laid on the stone ledge were hats forgotten or thrown away. She had grown quite attached to a green one that had lost its ribbons.

The instructor asked to be brought to the souvenir shop. He bought a glass ornament and a collar for his dog. On the way back a man at the petrol station gave one of the children a bird. They put it in the chapel. Made a nest for it. The servant threw it nest and all into the wastepaper basket. That night at supper the talk was of nothing else. He remembered his fish story and he told it to the new people who had come, how one morning he had to abandon his harpoon because the lines got tangled and next day, when he went back, he found that the shark had retreated into the cave and had two great lumps of rock in his mouth, where obviously he had bitten to free himself. That incident had a profound effect on him.

'Is the boat named after your mother?' she asked of his daughter. Her mother's name was Beth and the boat was called *Miss Beth*. 'He never said,' the daughter replied. She always disappeared after lunch. It must have been to accommodate them. Despite the heat they made a point of going to his room. And made a point of inventiveness. She tried a strong green stalk, to excite him, marveling at it, comparing him and it. He watched. He could not endure such competition. With her head upside down and close to the tiled floor she saw all the oils and ointments on his bathroom ledge and tried reading their labels backward. Do I like all this lovemaking? she asked herself. She had to admit that possibly she did not, that it went on too long, that it was involvement she sought, involvement and threat.

They swapped dreams. It was her idea. He was first. Everyone was careful to humor him. He said in a dream a dog was lost and his grief was great. He seemed to want to say more but didn't, or couldn't. Repeated the same thing, in fact. When it came to her turn, she told a different dream from the one she had meant to tell. A short, uninvolved little dream.

In the night she heard a guest sob. In the morning the same guest wore a flame dressing gown and praised the marmalade, which she ate sparingly.

She asked for the number of lessons to be increased. She had three a day and she did not go on the boat with the others. Between lessons she would walk along the shore. The pine trunks were pale, as if a lathe had been put to them. The winds of winter the lathe. In winter they would move; to catch up with friends, business meetings, art exhibitions, to buy presents, to shop. He hated suitcases, he liked clothes to be waiting wherever he went, and they were. She saw a wardrobe with his winter clothes neatly stacked, she saw his frieze cloak with the black astrakhan collar, and she experienced such a longing for that impossible season, that impossible city, and his bulk inside the cloak as they set out in the cold to go to a theater. Walking along the shore, she did the swimming movements in her head. It had got into all her thinking. Invaded her dreams. Atrocious dreams about her mother, her father, and one where lion cubs surrounded her as she lay on a hammock. The cubs were waiting to pounce the second she moved. The hammock, of course, was unsteady. Each time she wakened from one of those dreams she felt certain that her cries were the repeated cries of infancy, and it was then she helped herself to the figs she had brought up.

He put a handkerchief, folded like a letter, before her plate at table. On opening it she found some sprays of fresh mint, wide-leafed and cold. He had obviously put it in the refrigerator first. She smelled it and passed it around. Then on impulse she got up to kiss him and on her journey back nearly bumped into the servant with a tureen of soup, so excited was she.

Her instructor was her friend. 'We're winning, we're winning,' he said. He walked from dawn onward, walked the hills and saw the earth with dew on it. He wore a handkerchief on his head that he knotted over the ears, but as he approached the house, he removed this headdress. She met him on one of these morning walks. As it got nearer the time, she could neither sleep nor make love. 'We're winning, we're winning.' He always said it no matter where they met.

They set out to buy finger bowls. In the glass fac-
tory there were thin boys with very white skin who
secured pieces of glass with pokers and thrust
them into the stoves. The whole place smelled of
wood. There was chopped wood in piles, in corners.
Circular holes were cut along the top of the wall
between the square grated windows. The roof was
high and yet the place was a furnace. Five kittens
with tails like rats lay bunched immobile in a heap.
A boy, having washed himself in one of the available buckets of water, took the kittens one by one
and dipped them in. She took it to be an act of kind-
ness. Later he bore a hot blue bubble at the end of
a poker and laid it before her. As the flame subsid-
ed it became mauve, and as it cooled more, it was
almost colorless. It had the shape of a sea serpent
and an unnaturally long tail. Its color and its fin-
ished appearance were an accident, but the gift was
clearly intentioned. There was nothing she could
do but smile. As they were leaving she saw him

waiting near the motorcar, and as she got in, she waved wanly. That night they had asparagus, which is why they went to the trouble to get finger bowls. These were blue with small bubbles throughout, and though the bubbles may have been a defect, they gave to the thick glass an airiness.

There was a new dog, a mongrel, in whom he took no interest. He said the servants got new dogs simply because he allotted money for that. But as they were not willing to feed more than one animal, the previous year's dog was either murdered or put out on the mountain. All these dogs were of the same breed, part wolf; she wondered if when left on the mountain they reverted to being wolves. He said solemnly to the table at large that he would never allow himself to become attached to another dog. She said to him directly, 'Is it possible to know beforehand?' He said, 'Yes.' She could see that she had irritated him.

———

He came three times and afterward coughed badly. She sat with him and stroked his back, but when the coughing took command he moved her away. He leaned forward, holding a pillow to his mouth. She saw a film of his lungs, orange shapes with insets of dark that boded ill. She wanted to do some simple domestic thing like give him medicine, but he sent her away. Going back along the terrace, she could hear the birds. The birds were busy with their song. She met the fat woman. 'You have been derouted,' the woman said, 'and so have I.' And they bowed mockingly.

An archaeologist had been on a dig where a wooden temple was discovered. 'Tell me about your temple,' she said.

'I would say it's 400 B.C.,' he said, nothing more. Dry, dry.

A boy who called himself Jasper and wore mauve shirts received letters under the name of John. The letters were arranged on the hall table, each person's under a separate stone. Her mother wrote to say they were anxiously awaiting the good news. She said she hoped they would get engaged first but admitted that she was quite prepared to be told that the marriage had actually taken place. She knew how unpredictable he was. Her mother managed a poultry farm in England and was a compulsive eater.

Young people came to ask if Clay Sickle was staying at the house. They were in rags, but it looked as if they were rags worn on purpose and for effect. Their shoes were bits of motor tire held up with string. They all got out of the car, though the question could have been asked by any one of them. He was on his way back from the pool, and after two minutes' conversation he invited them for supper. He throve on new people. That night they were the ones in the limelight – the three unkempt boys and the long-haired girl. The girl had very striking eyes, which she fixed on one man and then another. She was determined to compromise one of them. The boys described their holiday, being broke, the trouble they had with the car, which was owned by a hire purchase firm in London. After dinner an incident occurred. The girl followed one of the men into the bathroom. 'Want to see what you've got there,' she said, and insisted on watching while the man peed. She said they would do any kind of fucking he wanted. She said he would be a slob not to try. It was too late to send them away, because earlier on they'd been invited to spend the night and beds were put up, down in the linen room. The girl was the last to go over there. She started a song, 'All around his cock he wears a tricolored rash-eo,' and she went on yelling it as she crossed the courtyard and went down the steps, brandishing a bottle.

In the morning, she determined to swim by herself. It was not that she mistrusted her instructor, but the time was getting closer and she was desperate. As she went to the pool, one of the youths appeared in borrowed white shorts, eating a banana. She greeted him with faltering gaiety. He said it was fun to be out before the others. He had a big head with closely cropped hair, a short neck, and a very large nose.

'Beaches are where I most want to be, where it all began,' he said. She thought he was referring to creation, and upon hearing such a thing he laughed profanely. 'Let's suppose there's a bunch of kids and you're all horsing around with a ball and all your sensory dimensions are working . . .'

'What?' she said.

'A hard-on . . .'

'Oh. . .'

'Now the ball goes into the sea and I follow and she follows me and takes the ball from my hand and a dense rain of energy, call it love, from me to her and vice versa, reciprocity in other words . . .'

Sententious idiot. She thought, Why do people like that have to be kept under his roof? Where is his judgment, where? She walked back to the house, furious at having to miss her chance to swim.

Dear Mother: It's not that kind of relationship. Being unmarried installs me as positively as being married, and neither installs me with any certainty. It is a beautiful house, but staying here

is quite a strain. You could easily get filleted.
Friends do it to friends. The food is good. Others
cook it, but I am responsible for each day's menu.
Shopping takes hours. The shops have a special
smell that is impossible to describe. They are all
dark, so that the foodstuffs won't perish. An old
woman goes along the street in a cart selling
fish. She has a very penetrating cry. It is like the
commencement of a song. There are always six
or seven little girls with her, they all have pierced
ears and wear fine gold sleepers. Flies swarm
around the cart even when it is upright in the
square. Living off scraps and fish scales, I expect.
We do not buy from her, we go to the harbor
and buy directly from the fishermen. The guests
– all but one woman – eat small portions. You
would hate it. All platinum people. They have a
canny sense of self-preservation; they know how
much to eat, how much to drink, how far to go;
you would think they invented somebody like
Shakespeare, so proprietary are they about his
genius. They are not fools – not by any means.

There is a chessboard of ivory and it is so large it stands on the floor. Seats of the right height are stationed around it.

Far back – in my most distant childhood, Mother – I remember your nightly cough; it was a lament really and I hated it. At the time I had no idea that I hated it, which goes to show how unreliable feelings are. We do not know what we feel at the time and that is very perplexing. Forgive me for mentioning the cough, it is simply that I think it is high time we spoke our minds on all matters. But don't worry. You are centuries ahead of the people here. In a nutshell, they brand you as idiot if you are harmless. There are jungle laws which you never taught me; you couldn't, you never knew them. Ah well!

I will bring you a present. Probably something suede. He says the needlework here is appalling and that things fall to pieces, but you can always have it remade. We had some nice china jelly molds when I was young. Whatever happened to them? Love.

Like the letter to the doctor, it was not posted. She didn't tear it up or anything, it just lay in an envelope and she omitted to post it from one day to the next. This new tendency disturbed her. This habit of postponing everything. It was as if something vital had first to be gone through. She blamed the swimming.

The day the pool was emptied she missed her three lessons. She could hear the men scrubbing, and from time to time she walked down and stood over them as if her presence could hurry the proceedings and make the water flow in, in one miracle burst. He saw how she fretted, he said they should have had two pools built. He asked her to come with them on the boat. The books and the suntan oil were as she had last seen them. The cliffs as intriguing as ever. 'Hello, cliff, can I fall off you?' She waved merrily. In a small harbor they saw another millionaire with his girl. They were alone, without even a crew. And for some reason it went straight to her heart. At dinner the men took bets as to who the girl was. They commented on her prettiness though they had hardly seen her. The water filling the pool sounded like a stream from a faraway hill. He said it would be full by morning.

Other houses had beautiful objects, but theirs was in the best taste. The thing she liked most was the dull brass chandelier from Portugal. In the evenings when it was lit, the cones of light tapered toward the rafters and she thought of woodsmoke and the wings of birds endlessly fluttering. Votive. To please her he had a fire lit in a far-off room simply to have the smell of woodsmoke in the air.

The watercress soup that was to be a specialty tasted like salt water. Nobody blamed her, but afterward she sat at the table and wondered how it had gone wrong. She felt defeated. On request he brought another bottle of red wine, but asked if she was sure she ought to have more. She thought, He does not understand the workings of my mind. But then, neither did she. She was drunk. She held the glass out. Watching the meniscus, letting it tilt from side to side, she wondered how drunk she would be when she stood up. 'Tell me,' she said, 'what interests you?' It was the first blunt question she had ever put to him.

'Why, everything,' he said.

'But deep down,' she said.

'Discovery,' he said, and walked away.

But not self-discovery, she thought, not that.

A neurologist got drunk and played jazz on the chapel organ. He said he could not resist it, there were so many things to press. The organ was stiff from not being used.

She retired early. Next day she was due to swim for them. She thought he would come to visit her. If he did they would lie in one another's arms and talk. She would knead his poor worn scrotum and ask questions about the world beneath the sea where he delved each day, ask about those depths and if there were flowers of some sort down there, and in the telling he would be bound to tell her about himself. She kept wishing for the organ player to fall asleep. She knew he would not come until each guest had retired, because he was strangely reticent about his loving.

But the playing went on. If anything, the player gathered strength and momentum. When at last he did fall asleep, she opened the shutters. The terrace lights were all on. The night breathlessly still. Across the fields came the lap from the sea and then the sound of a sheep bell, tentative and intercepted. Even a sheep recognized the dead of night. The lighthouse worked faithfully as a heartbeat. The dog lay in the chair, asleep, but with his ears raised. On other chairs were sweaters and books and towels, the remains of the day's activities. She watched and she waited. He did not come. She lamented that she could not go to him on the night she needed him most.

For the first time she thought about cramp.

In the morning she took three headache pills and swallowed them with hot coffee. They disintegrated in her mouth. Afterward she washed them down with soda water. There was no lesson because the actual swimming performance was to be soon after breakfast. She tried on one bathing suit, then another; then, realizing how senseless this was, she put the first one back on and stayed in her room until it was almost time.

When she came down to the pool they were all there ahead of her. They formed quite an audience: the twenty house guests and the six complaining children who had been obliged to quit the pool. Even the housekeeper stood on the stone seat under the tree, to get a view. Some smiled, some were a trifle embarrassed. The pregnant woman gave her a medal for good luck. It was attached to a pin. So they were friends. Her instructor stood near the front, the rope coiled around his wrist just in case. The children gave to the occasion its only levity. She went down the ladder backward and looked at no face in particular. She crouched until the water covered her shoulders, then she gave a short leap and delivered herself to it. Almost at once she knew that she was going to do it. Her hands, no longer loath to delve deep, scooped the water away, and she kicked with a ferocity she had not known to be possible. She was aware of cheering but it did not matter about that. She swam, as she had promised, across the width of the pool in the shallow end. It was pathetically short, but it was what she had vouched to do. Afterward one of the children said that her face was tortured. The rubber flowers had long since come off her bathing cap, and she pulled it off as she stood up and held on to the ladder. They clapped. They said it called for a celebration. He said nothing, but she could see that he was pleased. Her instructor was the happiest person there.

When planning the party they went to the study, where they could sit and make lists. He said they would order gypsies and flowers and the caviar would be served in glass swans packed with ice. None of it would be her duty. They would get people to do it. In all, they wrote out twenty telegrams. He asked how she felt. She admitted that being able to swim bore little relation to not being able. They were two unreconcilable feelings. The true thrill, she said, was the moment when she knew she would master it but had not yet achieved it with her body. He said he looked forward to the day when she went in and out of the water like a knife. He did the movement deftly with his hand. He said next thing she would learn was riding. He would teach her himself or he would have her taught. She remembered the chest-nut mare with head raised, nostrils sniffing the air, and she herself unable to stroke it, unable to stand next to it without exuding fear.

'Are you afraid of nothing?' she asked, too afraid to tell him specifically about the encounter with the mare, which took place in his stable.

'Sure, sure.'

'You never reveal it.'

'At the time I'm too scared.'

'But afterward, afterward . . .' she said.

'You try to live it down,' he said, and looked at her and hurriedly took her in his arms. She thought, Probably he is as near to me as he has been to any living person and that is not very near, not very near at all. She knew that if he chose her they would not go in the deep end, the deep end that she dreaded and dreamed of. When it came to matters inside himself, he took no risks.

She was tired. Tired of the life she had elected to go into and disappointed with the man she had put pillars around. The tiredness came from inside, and like a deep breath going out slowly, it tore at her gut. She was sick of her own predilection for tyranny. It seemed to her that she always held people to her ear, the way her mother held eggs, shaking them to guess at their rottenness, but unlike her mother she chose the very ones that she would have been wise to throw away. He seemed to sense her sadness, but he said nothing; he held her and squeezed her from time to time in reassurance.

Her dress – his gift – was laid out on the bed, its wide white sleeves hanging down at either side. It was of openwork and it looked uncannily like a corpse. There was a shawl to go with it, and shoes and a bag. The servant was waiting. Beside the bath her book, an ashtray, cigarettes, and a little book of soft matches that were hard to strike. She lit a cigarette and drew on it heartily. She regretted not having brought up a drink. She felt like a drink at that moment, and in her mind she sampled the drink she might have had. The servant knelt down to put in the stopper. She asked that the bath should not be run just yet. Then she took the biggest towel and put it over her bathing suit and went along the corridor and down by the back stairs. She did not have to turn on the lights; she would have known her way blindfolded to that pool. All the toys were on the water, like farm animals just put to bed. She picked them out one by one and laid them at the side near the pile of empty chlorine bottles. She went down the ladder backward.

She swam in the shallow end and allowed the dreadful thought to surface. She thought, I shall do it or I shall not do it, and the fact that she was of two minds about it seemed to confirm her view of the unimportance of the whole thing. Anyone, even the youngest child, could have persuaded her not to, because her mind was without conviction. It just seemed easier, that was all, easier than the strain and the incomplete loving and the excursions that lay ahead.

'This is what I want, this is where I want to go,' she said, restraining that part of herself that might scream. Once she went deep, and she submitted to it, the water gathered all around in a great beautiful bountiful baptism. As she went down to the cold and thrilling region she thought, They will never know, they will never, ever know, for sure.

At some point she began to fight and thresh about, and she cried, though she could not know the extent of those cries.

She came to her senses on the ground at the side of the pool, all muffled up and retching. There was an agonizing pain in her chest, as if a shears were snipping at her guts. The servants were with her and two of the guests and him. The floodlights were on around the pool. She put her hands to her breast to make sure; yes, she was naked under the blanket. They would have ripped her bathing suit off. He had obviously been the one to give respiration, because he was breathing quickly and his sleeves were rolled up. She looked at him. He did not smile. There was the sound of music, loud, ridiculous, and hearty. She remembered first the party, then everything. The nice vagueness quit her and she looked at him with shame. She looked at all of them. What things had she shouted as they brought her back to life? What thoughts had they spoken in those crucial moments? How long did it take? Her immediate concern was that they must not carry her to the house, she must not allow that last episode of indignity. But they did. As she was borne along by him and the gardener, she could see the flowers and the oysters and the jellied dishes and the small roast piglets all along the tables, a feast as in a dream, except that she was dreadfully clearheaded. Once alone in her room she vomited.

For two days she did not appear downstairs. He sent up a pile of books, and when he visited her he always brought someone. He professed a great interest in the novels she had read and asked how the plots were. When she did come down, the guests were polite and offhand and still specious, but along with that they were cautious now and deeply disapproving. Their manner told her that it had been a stupid and ghastly thing to do, and had she succeeded she would have involved all of them in her stupid and ghastly mess. She wished she could go home, without any farewells. The children looked at her and from time to time laughed out loud. One boy told her that his brother had once tried to drown him in the bath. Apart from that and the inevitable letter to the gardener, it was never mentioned. The gardener had been the one to hear her cry and raise the alarm. In their eyes he would be a hero.

People swam less. They made plans to leave. They had ready-made excuses – work, the change in the weather, airplane bookings. He told her that they would stay until all the guests had gone and then they would leave immediately. His secretary was traveling with them. He asked each day how she felt, but when they were alone, he either read or played patience. He appeared to be calm except that his eyes blazed as with fever. They were young eyes. The blue seemed to sharpen in color once the anger in him was resurrected. He was snappy with the servants. She knew that when they got back to London there would be separate cars waiting for them at the airport. It was only natural. The house, the warm flagstones, the shimmer of the water would sometimes, no doubt, reoccur to her; but she would forget him and he would live somewhere in the attic of her mind, the place where failure lurks.